Nick Ford Mysteries

The Secret of
Old Mexico

by
Jerry Stemach

in consultation with
Rene Ocaña,
Past Director,
Archeological Rescue Teams in Mexico

Don Johnston Incorporated
Volo, Illinois

Edited by:

Jerry Stemach, MS, CCC-SLP
AAC Specialist, Adaptive Technology Center, Sonoma County, California

Gail Portnuff Venable, MS, CCC-SLP
Speech-Language Pathologist, Scottish Rite Center for Childhood Language Disorders, San Francisco, California

Dorothy Tyack, MA
Learning Disabilities Specialist, Scottish Rite Center for Childhood Language Disorders, San Francisco, California

Consultant:

Ted S. Hasselbring, PhD
Professor of Special Education, Vanderbilt University, Nashville, TN

Cover Design and Illustration: Jeff Hamm, Karyl Shields

Interior Illustrations: Jeff Hamm

Published by:

Don Johnston Incorporated
26799 West Commerce Drive
Volo, IL 60073

DON JOHNSTON

International Standard Book Number
ISBN 1-893376-42-7

Contents

**This book is for
Uncle Leo.
No one told stories
like Uncle Leo.**

Many people have contributed to
The Secret of Old Mexico.
My wife, Beverly, my daughters, Kristie and Sarah
My friends and colleagues
Gail Portnuff Venable and Dorothy Tyack
Alan Venable
Rachel Whitaker
Rene Ocaña
The entire staff at Don Johnston Incorporated
TK Audio
Hacienda Mariposa
Kevin Feldman
Michael Benedetti, Michael Sturgeon, Melia Dicker
Robert Berta, photographer
and the good people of Michoacán, Mexico.

Chapter 1

Digging in the Jungle

Jeff Ford was standing in a deep, wide hole. Jeff and his best friend, Ken Rice, had dug the hole in the jungle in Yucatán, Mexico.

Jeff called to Ken, who was climbing down a ladder into the hole. "You'd better check this out," said Jeff.

Ken looked down at Jeff. Jeff was pointing at something in the dirt. Ken went down the ladder and stood next to him. Ken brushed away more of the dirt. Then Ken yelled. When he yelled, the monkeys in the jungle started to scream.

Ken looked up at the top of the hole. It was ten feet above his head. Next to the hole he could see big gray stones. The stones were part of a wall from an old temple. Plants with giant leaves hung over the stones. They covered the sides of the hole. The monkeys were screaming so loud that it was hard to hear.

Ken yelled again. "Doctor Gómez! Hector! Come quick! Jeff has found something!"

In less than a minute, two men were standing at the top of the hole and looking down at Ken and Jeff. One of the men was Dr. Carlos Gómez. He was a history teacher at City College of New York. He studied ancient history. He spent his summers looking for artifacts like tools, bowls, and statues that were made hundreds or thousands of years ago.

The government of Mexico had asked Dr. Gómez to explore the old temple in the Yucatán jungle.

The temple had been built about 1,500 years before by ancient Mayan people.

Dr. Gómez was a good friend of Jeff's dad, Nick. Nick Ford taught biology at City College. Dr. Gómez had asked Nick to help him in Mexico, but Nick was too busy, so Jeff and Ken got the job.

The other man was Hector Perez. He owned an art gallery in New York City that sold artifacts from Mexico and South America.

Dr. Gómez had hired Hector, Ken, and Jeff to help him dig up the ground next to the temple. They were searching for ancient Mayan artifacts.

Hector and Dr. Gómez climbed down the ladder. Jeff pointed again at the dirt. The men could see the top of an old round bowl that was made out of clay.

Dr. Gómez smiled. "This is what we have been looking for," he said.

Dr. Gómez unfolded a map of the hole. He made a mark to show the place where Jeff had found the bowl.

Then Dr. Gómez carefully brushed away the dirt and lifted the bowl out of the ground. Everyone stood close to Dr. Gómez.

"It has pictures on it," said Jeff.

"Those pictures tell an old story," said Dr. Gómez. "The bowl was found very deep in the hole, so we know that it is at least 1,000 years old. It may be even older than that."

"Wow," said Ken. "What do the pictures mean?"

Dr. Gómez turned the bowl slowly in his hands. He said, "The pictures show that an important artifact was taken out of this temple and carried to another temple that is far away from here."

Hector looked at the pictures, too. He smiled. "You are right, Dr. Gómez," said Hector. "And I know just what it was."

Chapter 2

The Secret Map

Later that day, after dinner, Jeff and Ken sat around the campfire with Hector and Dr. Gómez. Jeff looked at Hector and said, "I'm ready for a good story. Tell us about the pictures on that bowl. Tell us what was taken from here."

"It was a Chac-mool," said Hector.

"What's a Chac-mool?" asked Ken.

" 'Chac-mool' is an old Mayan word," said Hector. "It means 'messenger of god.' A Chac-mool is a special statue.

The Mayan people believed that a Chac-mool could talk with the gods in heaven."

Hector took a small book out of his pocket. He opened the book to a page that showed a picture of a small statue. The statue looked like a person who was lying down. Hector passed the book around to the others.

Dr. Gómez spoke. "The bowl that Jeff found is like a map from a long time ago. The pictures on the bowl will tell us where the Chac-mool was taken."

"It sure must be an important Chac-mool," said Ken. "Some dude went to a lot of trouble to paint a road map on that bowl."

Dr. Gómez smiled. "We are in a part of the Yucatán called Chichén Itzá. This place was important to the Mayan people because they believed that the Rain God made special water here. The word 'chichén' means 'a well.' "

"Do you mean like a well in the ground filled with water?" asked Jeff.

"Yes," said Dr. Gómez. "People prayed to the Rain God and then they threw a gift down into the well. Mayan people came here from all over Mexico and Central America. A few years ago, someone found gold down at the bottom of the well."

Hector spoke. "I wish that I had been the one who dug up that well."

"What a waste," said Ken. "If I'd lived back then, I would have put my gold in a bank."

Dr. Gómez laughed at Ken. "If you'd lived back then, you would have thrown your gold down the well, also," said Dr. Gómez. "You would have wanted to make the gods happy."

Hector said, "When Mayan people died, they were buried under their houses. Their families kept on living in the houses."

"That would give me the creeps," said Ken.

"The Mayan people didn't think that death was creepy," said Hector.

"The Mayan people believed that when you died, you went to live in the sky. You became a star."

Jeff looked up at the sky. Then he said, "I might want to become a baseball star."

Ken laughed. "Hey Jeff," said Ken. "If you were any good at *basketball*, you could become a shooting star!" Everyone laughed.

Jeff spoke again. "I'm glad I live right now. I need my books, TV, and baseball."

Dr. Gómez said, "The Mayans also played ball. Their game was a little like basketball. About 1,000 years ago, they built the biggest ball field in this part of the world."

"Did they have teams and stuff?" asked Ken.

"No," said Dr. Gómez. "We think that they played ball to find out who would be the next person to be killed and given to the gods."

Chapter 3

Mr. Morris

Dr. Gómez stood up from the campfire. "It's after midnight and I think that we should get some sleep," he said. "Tomorrow morning, Hector and I will study the pictures on the bowl. I want you boys to call Nick and tell him about this. Maybe Nick, Kris, and Mandy can come to Mexico and help us."

Both boys grinned. Kris Ford was Jeff's sister and Mandy Ming was Kris's best friend. Jeff and Ken and the girls were all students at City College of New York.

The four kids went on many trips with Nick Ford. But now Jeff and Ken were on this trip alone. They had not seen Kris and Mandy for three weeks.

"I'll call them right now!" shouted Ken.

Dr. Gómez smiled. "Ken, I know that you and Jeff can't wait to see the girls," he said. "But it's midnight here. That means that it's 1 o'clock in the morning in New York. It's way too late for any phone calls. Let's all get to bed."

Hector picked up the bowl. "I'll take good care of this baby until tomorrow," he said. "I will lock it up in the toolbox in the big tent. Then I'll grab my sleeping bag and sleep there, too. I don't want anything to happen to this bowl."

Ken smiled at Jeff. Then Ken said to Hector, "Don't let the snakes bite you, Hector."

Dr. Gómez did not laugh. "Yes, Hector. You be careful. The jungle is full of dangerous snakes and spiders," said Dr. Gómez.

When Hector got to the big tent, he lit a lantern. Then he zipped up the door of the tent. "I don't want any visitors tonight," he said to himself.

Hector opened a box that was filled with books. He took out a big book and laid it on a table next to the bowl and lantern. After studying the book and the bowl, Hector took out his cell phone. He punched a number into it and then he turned off the lantern. The phone rang many times before someone answered it.

At last a tired voice spoke. "Hello? Hello? Who is this?" the voice asked.

Hector laughed and said, "Good morning, Mr. Morris! This is Hector Perez. I have some good news for you!"

Mr. Morris sounded upset. "Hector?" he said. "It's 3 o'clock in the morning and you woke me up! What do you want?"

Hector spoke softly. "*I* don't want anything, Mr. Morris. But maybe I have something that *you* want.

I have a nice Chac-mool for your collection," said Hector.

"I don't need another Chac-mool," said Mr. Morris. "You already sold me a Chac-mool."

Hector spoke again. "Listen to me, Mr. Morris. I will only say this once. In one week, I will have a Chac-mool that is made out of pure gold. It will be worth millions of dollars. Now do you want another Chac-mool or not?" asked Hector.

Mr. Morris was wide awake now. "Yes! Yes, you know that I want it," said Mr. Morris. "Who else knows about this?"

"No one else knows that it is made out of pure gold," said Hector.

"How much money do you want?" asked Mr. Morris.

"$100,000 for now," said Hector. "Send $100,000 to my art gallery as soon as the bank opens tomorrow morning. Then maybe I won't think about selling it to someone else," said Hector.

"No, Hector," said Mr. Morris. "I will send you $150,000. But if you sell this Chac-mool to anyone else, you will be a dead man, my friend."

Hector pushed a button on his cell phone to end the call. "Morris doesn't scare me," said Hector to himself. Hector unrolled his sleeping bag. He checked for spiders and snakes before he got into the bag and went to sleep.

Chapter 4

Help on the Way

The next morning, Ken got up early. He found his own cell phone, and called Nick and Kris Ford in New York City. Nick answered the phone. Ken told Nick about the discovery of the bowl and the plan to find the Chac-mool.

"Gee, Ken," said Nick. "It sure sounds exciting! I would love to help you, but I'm on my way to San Francisco. There is a new Museum of Latin Culture that will open there in a few weeks. I'm helping them get the museum ready to open."

Kris Ford was listening to her dad. She picked up another phone in their apartment and spoke to Ken. "Mandy and I would love to help you," Kris said.

Nick laughed. "OK, OK, so who needs me, anyway?" he asked.

All that day, Nick helped Kris and Mandy get ready for the trip to Mexico. First, they took a taxi to Hector's art gallery. The gallery was in a part of New York City called Manhattan.

They went into the gallery and
spoke to a man named Luis. Nick told
Luis that Kris and Mandy were going to
Mexico to help Hector and Dr. Gómez.

Luis showed the girls a map of
Mexico and the Yucatán. Then he
showed them some of the artifacts in
the gallery. "Some of these artifacts
were made thousands of years ago.
They all come from Mexico and Central
America," said Luis. "You girls will be
helping Dr. Gómez and Hector find an
important Mayan artifact."

Before Nick and the girls left, Luis handed Kris a plain white envelope. "Will you please give this to Hector for me?" Luis asked. "There are some important papers inside."

Kris took the envelope from Luis and promised that she would give it to Hector.

Chapter 5

The Money

After they left the art gallery, Nick and the girls went to the Bank of New York. Mandy and Kris each took some money out of their savings accounts. The bank teller handed each girl an envelope with $150 inside.

Nick spoke to the girls. "Now we need to change some of your American money into Mexican money. In the United States, we use dollars to buy things, but in Mexico, they use money called *pesos*," Nick explained.

"We will go to another bank called the Exchange Bank. The people at that bank will sell you pesos."

The girls and Nick walked to the Exchange Bank. Kris handed her envelope of money to the teller. "My friend and I are going to Mexico," said Kris. "We want to buy some pesos. Here is $150."

The teller spoke to Kris in Spanish. *"No problema, señorita,"* he said. The teller opened the envelope. Then he looked at Kris, Mandy, and Nick.

The teller spoke in English. "There must be a mistake," he said. The man held up a paper. "This is not $150. This is a check for $150,000."

Nick and Mandy and Kris looked at the paper that the man was holding. It was a bank check for $150,000! The check was made out to Hector Perez.

"That's not mine," said Kris. "I gave you the wrong envelope."

Nick spoke. "Maybe Hector is buying more art for his gallery," he said.

The bank teller handed the check back to Mandy. "You'd better keep this in a safe place," he said.

Back in Mexico, Dr. Gómez, Hector, and the boys were studying a map of the country.

Hector was pointing to a blue dot on the map. "That is where we must go," said Hector. "That blue dot on the map is Lake Pátzcuaro."

"There is an old temple near there called 'Tzintzuntzan,' " said Hector.

"Cool name," said Jeff.

"The word 'Tzintzuntzan' means 'hummingbird,'" said Dr. Gómez.

"That little bird gets really big names," said Ken.

Hector spoke again. "The pictures on the bowl say that a special Chac-mool was carried to the temple at Tzintzuntzan."

"It looks like it's a long way from here," said Jeff.

"Yes," said Hector. "It's more than 1,000 miles."

"That was some hike," said Ken. "I don't even want to *drive* that far in the Jeep!"

"Here's the plan," said Hector. "I know that Kris and Mandy are coming to help us. But we'll need more help than that to find the Chac-mool. So I will fly to Pátzcuaro today and hire some Indians to help us look for the Chac-mool. You stay here and pack up our tools and equipment. It will take you three days to drive to Pátzcuaro."

Dr. Gómez spoke. "I am glad that you are here, Hector, because you always know just what to do."

Chapter 6

A New Heart

Ken drove Hector to the airport. Jeff and Dr. Gómez started packing up their equipment. Jeff was working in the tent where Hector had slept the night before. Just as Jeff started to pick up a box, he saw something move. He looked up. A snake was hanging from a rope right in front of Jeff's face! The snake was about two feet long and it was red, yellow, and black. Jeff stood still and called to Dr. Gómez. "There's a snake in here and I think it wants to bite me," said Jeff.

Dr. Gómez opened the tent flap. He was holding a shovel. He lifted the shovel between Jeff and the snake and knocked the snake to the ground. The snake crawled through the flap and into the jungle. "It's a coral snake!" yelled Dr. Gómez. "A bite from that snake would be the kiss of death."

Jeff jumped back. "Hector was lucky last night," he said.

"Yes," said Dr. Gómez. "Hector is always lucky."

By now, Hector was in Pátzcuaro. He went to the plaza in the middle of town. There was a beautiful fountain in the plaza where many Indians were selling fresh fruit, clothes, and pottery. Hector spoke to a man who was selling fruit. The man's wife was sitting next to him. She was holding a little girl on her lap.

Hector spoke to the man and woman in Spanish. "You have a pretty little girl," said Hector.

The man looked sad. He shook his head and said, "Thank you, *señor*, but my little girl is sick. The doctor says that she needs a heart operation or she will die. I don't have enough pesos to pay for an operation."

Hector looked at the little girl. "Maybe I can help you," Hector told them. "I am here to dig a big hole near the old temple at Tzintzuntzan. If you help me, I will pay you $10,000. $10,000 can pay for your little girl's heart."

The man jumped up. *"Sí, señor! I am your man! We can go dig now! I will get my shovel!"*

Hector laughed. "Not so fast! First tell me your name," he said.

The man grinned. *"Ocho!"* he said. "My name is Ocho!"

"Ocho?" said Hector. "Ocho means 'eight' in Spanish. What kind of a name is that?"

"I have seven older sisters," said the man. "I am number eight. I am Ocho!"

Hector laughed again. "Maybe I will hire you, Ocho. But I will need at least 20 more men besides you. Can you find 20 more strong men to help us? Tell the men that I will pay $40 a week."

"$40 is a lot of money," said Ocho. "I can get more men right away."

Hector got closer to Ocho. Hector asked him, "Can you keep a secret, Ocho? You must not tell anyone about what we find at the temple.

You must not tell *your* friends and you must not tell *my* friends. If you tell anyone, I will not pay you, and your little girl will not get her new heart."

Chapter 7

Day of the Dead

Ken, Jeff, and Dr. Gómez arrived in Pátzcuaro after driving for three days. It was the Day of the Dead in Mexico and there were big celebrations everywhere. The men found Hector in the plaza. Ken said that he would drive one more hour to Morelia to pick up Kris and Mandy at the airport.

When the plane from New York landed, Ken was glad to see the girls again. The three kids got into the Jeep and drove back to Pátzcuaro. On the way, Ken told the girls about everything that had happened.

As they passed a graveyard, Ken slowed down. It was midnight, but there were many people visiting the graveyard. The people had placed hundreds of candles on the graves.

"What's going on?" asked Mandy.

"This is 'Day of the Dead' in Mexico," said Ken. "All the people here go to the graveyards and put out fresh flowers and food for the members of their families who have died. They stay here all night long. It's a big party," he said.

Mandy looked at all of the people standing by the graves. "It sounds creepy," said Mandy.

"People in Mexico don't think that graveyards are creepy," Ken told them. "In Mexico, people like to remember their family and friends who have died."

By the time Ken drove into Pátzcuaro, it was 1 o'clock in the morning. But it seemed like the middle of the day because there were people everywhere. Most of the people wore costumes. People were dancing and singing and eating and talking.

Ken parked the Jeep. "I told Jeff that we would meet him in the plaza by the fountain," he said.

They all got out of the car.

Kris looked around at the crowds. "Wow," she said. "This is some party!"

"Maybe we can find something to eat," said Mandy. "I'm starving!"

Kris, Mandy, and Ken started to walk toward the fountain. Suddenly, two men ran up to them. One man was dressed in a devil costume. The other man was dressed like a skeleton.

Kris screamed. Ken turned to look at her. Then he started to laugh. The two men were Jeff and Hector. Jeff took off his mask.

"Hello, little sister!" Jeff said to Kris.

"I hate you, Jeff," said Kris. "You scared me to death!"

Jeff hugged both girls. Then he said, "Kris and Mandy, I want you to meet Hector Perez. Hector is not really a devil. He's just dressed up like one."

Hector shook hands with the girls. "It's nice to meet you," he said. Then he asked, "Did you bring a letter for me?"

Kris looked at Mandy. "Yes," said Mandy. "I have it right here."

Mandy handed the envelope to Hector. Hector walked off by himself to look at it.

Jeff spoke. "It must be something important," he said.

Mandy said, "It's important, all right. It's a bank check for $150,000."

Ken shook his head. "That's a big pile of pesos in Mexico," he said.

"Why would Hector need that much money in Mexico?" asked Jeff. Jeff looked for Hector in the crowd, but he had disappeared!

Chapter 8

Bad Luck

The next morning, Dr. Gómez took everyone to the temple at Tzintzuntzan. Hector and Ocho and many other men were already there. Hector was pounding stakes into the ground and tying string between the stakes to show the men where to dig.

Dr. Gómez said 'Good morning' to the men in Spanish. *"Buenos días,"* he said.

"Buenos días," said the men.

Dr. Gómez spoke to Hector. "I was just telling Kris and Mandy that if we dig up an artifact, we must give it to the government. It's against the law to take it out of Mexico."

"Yes, yes, that's right," said Hector. Then he laughed and said, "Don't put anything in your pockets except your hands!"

Ken spoke. "Well, Hector, we're ready for work. How can we help?"

Hector handed Ken a piece of paper. "You kids can drive to the plaza and buy this list of supplies."

Dr. Gómez looked at the list. "I'll go with them," he said. "They may need me to speak Spanish for them."

The kids and Dr. Gómez drove back into town. Then they walked around the plaza, looking for the supplies on Hector's list. Suddenly, Dr. Gómez saw an old Chac-mool on an Indian's blanket. He bent down to look at it.

Dr. Gómez pointed at the Chac-mool. "Is that for sale?" he asked. *"Sí, señor.* 200 pesos," said the Indian.

"I think that's about $18," Kris said to Mandy.

Dr. Gómez counted out 200 pesos and paid the Indian. The Indian handed the Chac-mool to Dr. Gómez.

"Where did you find this?" Mandy asked the Indian. The Indian spoke in Spanish and it was too fast for Mandy to understand.

"He said that he found it in his field," said Dr. Gómez. "He owns a small farm by the temple."

"Is this the Chac-mool that we are looking for?" asked Mandy.

"I don't think so," said Dr. Gómez. "This Chac-mool is old, but it doesn't look special. I bought it for three reasons. First, that poor Indian needs the money. Second, I want the Indians at the temple to see it. Then they will know the kind of artifact that we are looking for."

"What's the third reason?" asked Jeff.

Dr. Gómez patted the statue. "I will give this to the government so that they can put it in a museum.

If I don't buy it, someone else will buy it and sneak it out of Mexico."

Dr. Gómez and the kids drove back to the temple. When Dr. Gómez showed the Chac-mool to the Indians, they looked upset.

"What's the matter?" asked Kris.

Hector spoke. "They say that digging up a Chac-mool is bad luck."

"Why is it bad luck?" asked Kris.

"They think that a Chac-mool has special power," said Hector. "They think that they might get sick if they dig one up."

"That's silly," said Mandy.

"Well, there are stories," said Dr. Gómez.

"What kind of stories?" asked Ken.

Dr. Gómez looked at Hector. Then he looked at Ken and said, "Some people have died after opening up old graves near temples."

Chapter 9

Thunder and Lightning

The next morning, Hector was ready to start digging. He had divided the ground next to the temple into squares. Each square was about three feet wide.

Dr. Gómez showed everyone how to dig up the dirt carefully a little bit at a time. He used spoons and brushes to take the dirt out of one of the squares.

"You must dig carefully. It will take you all day to dig down just 12 inches," said Dr. Gómez. "But when you dig down that far, you might find things that are 300 years old."

Next Dr. Gómez put one person in each square and everyone started to dig.

By 4 o'clock in the afternoon, all the holes were 12 inches deep. One man found a small bone. Kris dug up a peso coin that said 1922 on it. Ken uncovered a Coke bottle.

Then it began to rain. Jeff ran over to Ken. "Wow, Ken," yelled Jeff. "You found the 'Real Thing!' Maybe a Mayan king drank out of that Coke bottle 5,000 years ago."

Ken yelled back, "You're just mad because all that you found was dirt."

The rain was coming down hard, so Hector told everyone to go home.

Hector spoke to Ocho. "Tell the workers to be here at 6 o'clock in the morning."

Ocho smiled. "I can tell them to come at 6 o'clock," he said. "Maybe they will come at 8 o'clock. Maybe they will come at 9 o'clock."

Hector was angry. "If they come at 9 o'clock, I will fire them!" he said.

Ocho smiled again. *"Señor, you* tell them," he said. "They are my friends. They will work hard for you. But they have families. In the morning, they want to spend time with their families. Then they come to work for you."

Hector swore at Ocho and walked away.

The next day, it was too muddy to keep digging. Jeff and Ken helped Hector build a shed. Hector said that if they found a Chac-mool, he wanted to lock it up in the shed.

When the shed was finished, Hector put a strong lock on the door.

On the third day, everyone started digging again. At 2 o'clock, one of the Indians found a large Chac-mool that was made out of clay. Dr. Gómez lifted it up so that everyone could see it. Just as he lifted the Chac-mool, there was a flash of lightning and then a loud boom of thunder. Then lightning flashed again and it hit a tree. The tree was on fire!

The Indian workers were scared. They were sure that the Chac-mool was bringing bad luck. They all dropped their tools and walked quickly away.

"Come back here!" yelled Hector at the men. Then Hector yelled at Ocho. "Tell those men to come back!"

But Ocho just shook his head. "The men think that God is mad at us because we dug up the Chac-mool. Who do you think they will listen to?" asked Ocho. "Me or God?"

"Well then," said Hector, "we will keep digging by ourselves!"

Chapter 10

Stolen!

By 6 o'clock, Mandy and Dr. Gómez had found two more Chac-mools. Hector looked at each one carefully. Then he locked both of the Chac-mools in the shed.

At last, it was too dark to dig. The four kids got into their Jeep and drove back to their hotel.

"We found three Chac-mools today," Jeff said.

Ken stopped him. "What do you mean 'we?' " he said. "All you dug up was a pile of dirt."

"OK, OK," said Jeff. "But did you see Hector? He wasn't happy about finding any of them."

"Something's not right here," said Kris. "I don't trust Hector."

"Me either," said Mandy. "And I want to know why Hector got $150,000."

The next morning, Ken and Jeff went to the shed to get their tools for digging. When they got close to the shed, Jeff yelled, "Look!" The door was wide open and one of the Chac-mools was gone from the shelf!

Dr. Gómez ran over to Ken and Jeff. "Is everything OK?" asked Dr. Gómez.

"No," said Ken, shaking his head. "Someone has stolen one of our Chac-mools."

"Why would someone take only one of them?" asked Jeff.

Ken pointed at the shelf. "Check this out," he said. "There are bits of broken pottery on the shelf. Someone has chipped the bottom of each statue. Why would anyone do that?"

"I don't know," said Dr. Gómez. "There are some bits of broken pottery over here, too. These must be from the missing Chac-mool."

Dr. Gómez picked up the bits of pottery. Then he said, "Let's look at these under the microscope."

The boys followed Dr. Gómez back to the Jeep. Dr. Gómez took out his microscope and set it up on a table. He looked into the microscope.

"What are you looking at?" asked Mandy.

"I'm looking at trouble," said Dr. Gómez. "Take a look for yourself."

Mandy looked first. "Is that what I think it is?" she asked .

"Yes," said Dr. Gómez. "You are looking at tiny flakes of pure gold!" Dr. Gómez leaned back against the Jeep.

Mandy looked at him. "Are you OK, Dr. Gómez?" she asked. "You look as white as a ghost."

Dr. Gómez started to speak. "I feel very..." he said. Suddenly, Dr. Gómez closed his eyes and fainted!

Kris bent down to help him. "Quick!" she yelled. "Get Hector! Get Ocho! Dr. Gómez may be dying!"

"I'll find Hector," said Jeff. "Ken, you drive over to Ocho's house."

When Jeff came back, Dr. Gómez was sitting up. Mandy was giving him a drink of water.

"I looked everywhere," Jeff said. "Hector is gone!"

Just then, Ken and Ocho drove up in the Jeep. "OK," said Ken. "I got my man here, but I can't speak much Spanish."

Kris spoke to Ocho in Spanish. "Where is Hector?" she asked.

"San Pancho," answered Ocho. *"Boleto para San Pancho."*

Kris spoke to the others. "Ocho says that Hector went to San Pancho.

'Boleto' is the Spanish word for ticket. Hector got a ticket to San Pancho."

"Yes," said Ken. "And you can bet that there is a golden Chac-mool in his suitcase!"

Chapter 11

San Pancho

Kris asked Ocho about Hector and San Pancho. Ocho said that Hector left in the middle of the night. But Ocho did not know how to get to San Pancho.

"Did Hector give you anything?" asked Kris.

Ocho reached into his pocket. He pulled his hand out and smiled. Ocho was holding a pile of $100 bills. "Hector gave me this," said Ocho in Spanish. "Now my little girl can have a new heart."

Dr. Gómez sat up and asked Ocho about the Chac-mool.

"Hector took the Chac-mool with him," said Ocho. "Hector thinks that it is worth a lot of money."

Jeff spoke to Dr. Gómez. "Why was the gold Chac-mool hidden inside the clay pottery? How did Hector know that there was a gold Chac-mool at Tzintzuntzan?"

"Hector knew that it was gold from the pictures on the bowl," answered Dr. Gómez. "But he did not tell us. I fainted because that Chac-mool is covered with poison," said Dr. Gómez.

"When I touched some of the poison, it made me sick. Ocho says that I am lucky that it didn't kill me."

Ken was angry. "I'll bet Hector put that poison on there," he yelled. "If I catch that dude, I'll rub his nose in it."

Dr. Gómez held up his hand. "No. Hector did not put the poison on the Chac-mool. The people who lived here about 300 years ago did it to keep the Chac-mool safe. When the explorers came here from Spain, they wanted all of the gold in Mexico.

They wanted to take the gold back to the Queen of Spain."

"I still don't get why there was poison on the Chac-mool," said Jeff.

"I'm coming to that part," said Dr. Gómez. "The Chac-mool was important to the Mayan people who lived here. They wanted to hide it from the explorers, so they covered the Chac-mool with clay. Then they painted the clay with poison. They got the poison from plants. Then they dug a hole next to the temple and buried the Chac-mool in the ground."

"Now what?" asked Kris.

"Well," said Ken. "We'd better find Hector before that poison kills him!"

Kris and Mandy stood at the back of the Jeep, looking at a map of Mexico. Ken was talking to someone on his cell phone. Jeff walked over to them.

"Any luck?" asked Jeff.

Mandy spoke. "We have checked every map that we own," she said. "There is no place called San Pancho on any of them."

Just then, Ken hung up his cell phone and hollered, "San Pancho, here I come!"

"So where is San Pancho?" asked Jeff.

"I'll tell you later," said Ken. "The plane leaves in one hour. There is only one seat left and that seat's for me. I just hope that I won't be sitting next to Hector."

Mandy spoke. "We'll never make it," she said. "It takes an hour to drive to the airport from here."

Ken tossed the keys to Kris. "That's why I want Kris to drive. The woman puts the pedal to the metal!"

Chapter 12

In the Bag

Ken had just two minutes to get ready to go to the airport. He was yelling orders at everyone. "Jeff, go get a Chac-mool out of the shed and put it into my red gym bag. Kris, I need a pair of rubber gloves."

Next, Ken spoke to Mandy. "Mandy, find some kind of a costume that I can wear to fool Hector. I want all of you to be back here in two minutes! I'll grab my wallet and a cell phone."

Everyone was in the Jeep in less than two minutes. Kris put the Jeep in first gear and hit the gas. The tires squealed.

As Kris turned onto the main highway, Ken told the others about San Pancho. "I called the airport. They told me that San Pancho is just the Mexican name for San Francisco," he said. "Hector is taking the Chac-mool to San Francisco!"

"Ken!" said Kris. "I just remembered! My dad is in San Francisco right now.

He's staying at the Hilton Hotel. Let's call him up and tell him to meet the plane."

Ken took out the cell phone. He made a few phone calls to get the telephone number for the Hilton Hotel. Soon the phone in Nick Ford's hotel room was ringing. "Darn!" said Ken. "He's not there. I'll have to leave a message for him." Ken spoke into the cell phone. He said that Nick should go to the San Francisco airport and meet Ken's flight at gate 60. He told Nick that there could be trouble.

Kris drove fast. When she got to the airport, Ken grabbed his gym bag and jumped out. He started to run. The airplane was just leaving the gate. Kris ran after Ken. She yelled to a man in Spanish. The man picked up a phone while he quickly checked Ken's passport. Then the man opened a door and Ken ran out to the plane.

"He made it!" yelled Mandy.

"Yes," said Jeff. "But that's just the first problem. Now he needs to get past Hector."

When Ken got on the plane, the stewardess made him sit in a seat next to the door. "This is not your seat," she said. "But you must sit here until after we take off."

Ken was glad. That would give him time to put on the costume that Mandy got for him. When Ken opened his gym bag, he began to laugh. He took out a pair of sunglasses with thick, black frames. Then he took out a black wig, a dirty cowboy hat, and a jacket that said 'San Francisco Giants.'

"Where did Mandy get all of this stuff in just two minutes?" he asked himself.

After a while, the stewardess came back and spoke to Ken. "You are in seat 22-C," she told him. "It is safe for you to go to your seat now."

"That's what you think, lady," Ken said to himself. Ken got up and walked back toward his seat. He kept looking for Hector. Then Ken saw him! Hector was sitting in seat 23-C, the seat right behind Ken's seat!

Chapter 13

The Snake

As Ken sat down, he peeked at Hector. Hector's eyes were closed. "Hector looks sick," thought Ken.

Ken saw Hector's black bag under Ken's seat. "This is a good time to switch the Chac-mools," said Ken.

Ken slowly picked up Hector's bag. Ken unzipped his red gym bag and put on a pair of gloves. Next, he unzipped Hector's bag. When Ken looked into the bag, he nearly screamed! The golden Chac-mool was in the bag.

But next to the Chac-mool was a large snake! The snake was red and black and white. It hissed at Ken.

Ken closed the bag. His heart was pounding. He pushed the bag carefully back under the seat.

Ken got up and went back to the stewardess. "The man in seat 23-C is Hector Perez. He is my friend," Ken said. "But he is sick. He will need a wheelchair when we land in San Francisco."

"I will call the airport for one right away," said the stewardess.

Chapter 13   The Secret of Old Mexico   **113**

Ken went back to his seat and waited. "How do you sneak gold and a snake onto an airplane?" Ken asked himself.

When the plane landed, Ken lifted Hector into the wheelchair. Hector looked like he was dead. Ken put his red gym bag onto Hector's lap while the stewardess pushed the wheelchair into the airport.

A tall man walked over to the stewardess. "Excuse me," said the man. "My name is Mr. Morris. I am here to help Mr. Perez."

Hector opened his eyes a little and groaned. Mr. Morris picked up the gym bag and opened it.

Ken looked past the tall man and saw Nick Ford and a policeman. The policeman had a German Shepherd dog on a leash. Nick called to the man and said, "Mr. Morris! You are under arrest!"

The man started to run. He was still holding Ken's gym bag. The dog ran after him. It grabbed at Ken's bag and ripped it open.

The Chac-mool statue flew through the air and landed on the floor. The statue broke into a hundred pieces. The man groaned.

Ken and the policeman walked up to the man. Ken handed the man Hector's black bag. "I think that this is what you're looking for," said Ken.

The man opened the bag. Then he saw the snake and he dropped the bag. The policeman put handcuffs on Mr. Morris and Hector.

When the snake crawled out of the bag, some people screamed. Nick Ford walked over and picked up the snake.

"No, Nick!" yelled Ken. "That snake can kill you!"

Nick laughed. "I teach biology, remember? This isn't a Coral snake. It's a California mountain king snake. It doesn't bite people."

Nick picked up the bag with the gold Chac-mool inside. He handed it to another man. "Ken, I want you to meet Mr. Lopez. He is from Mexico City.

He is in San Francisco to open the
new Museum of Latin Culture."

Mr. Lopez shook hands with Ken.
"I want to thank you and your friends
for stopping these men. My
government wants to give the gold
Chac-mool to the new museum in
San Francisco. And we want all of
you to come to the celebration."

"That's great," said Ken. "We would
love to join you. Just promise me that
there won't be any snakes."

The End

A Note from the Start-to-Finish Editors

You will notice that Start-to-Finish Books look different from other high-low readers and chapter books. The text layout of this book coordinates with the other media components (CD and audiocassette) of the Start-to-Finish series.

The text in the book matches, line-for-line and page-for-page, the text shown on the computer screen, enabling readers to follow along easily in the book. Each page ends in a complete sentence so that the student can either practice the page (repeat reading) or turn the page to continue with the story. If the next sentence cannot fit on the page in its entirety, it has been shifted to the next page. For this reason, the sentence at the top of a page may not be indented, signaling that it is part of the paragraph from the preceding page.

Words are not hyphenated at the ends of lines. This sometimes creates extra space at the end of a line, but eliminates confusion for the struggling reader.